A Note to Parents

Reading books aloud and playing word games are two valuable ways parents can help their children learn to read. The easy-to-read stories in the **My First Hello Reader! With Flash Cards** series are designed to be enjoyed together. Six activity pages and 16 flash cards in each book help reinforce phonics, sight vocabulary, reading comprehension, and facility with language. Here are some ideas to develop your youngster's reading skills:

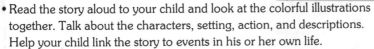

Reading with Your Child

- Read the story aloud to your child and look at the colorful illustrations together. Talk about the characters, setting, action, and descriptions. Help your child link the story to events in his or her own life.
- Read parts of the story and invite your child to fill in the missing parts. At first, pause to let your child "read" important last words in a line. Gradually, let your child supply more and more words or phrases. Then take turns reading every other line until your child can read the book independently.

Enjoying the Activity Pages

- Treat each activity as a game to be played for fun. Allow plenty of time to play.
- Read the introductory information aloud and make sure your child understands the directions.

Using the Flash Cards

- Read the words aloud with your child. Talk about the letters and sounds and meanings.
- Match the words on the flash cards with the words in the story.
- Help your child find words that begin with the same letter and sound, words that rhyme, and words with the same ending sound.
- Challenge your child to put flash cards together to make sentences from the story and create new sentences.

Above all else, make reading time together a fun time. Show your child that reading is a pleasant and meaningful activity. Be generous with your praise and know that, as your child's first and most important teacher, you are contributing immensely to his or her command of the printed word.

ISBN 0-590-25498-7
Copyright © 1995 by Nancy Hall, Inc.
All rights reserved. Published by Scholastic Inc.
CARTWHEEL BOOKS and the CARTWHEEL BOOKS logo
are registered trademarks of Scholastic Inc.
MY FIRST HELLO READER and the MY FIRST HELLO READER logo
are trademarks of Scholastic Inc.

12 11 10 9 8 7 6   9/9 0/0

24

Printed in the U.S.A.
First Scholastic printing, November 1995

I KNOW KARATE

by Mary Packard
Illustrated by Dee de Rosa

**My First Hello Reader!
With Flash Cards**

SCHOLASTIC INC.
New York Toronto London Auckland Sydney

I know karate.
See me bow?

I can block.

This is how.

See my stance?

See my gi?

I can jump.

Look at me!

See my form?

I can kick.

I can chop.

See how quick!

I	Hairy
know	at
karate	can
dog	block

fun	see
form	me
here	bow
big	scary

this	stance
is	how
a	chop
my	and

monster	jump
make	run
kick	*gi*
quick	look

Karate is fun.

I can make a monster run!

Here is a monster—
big and scary.

Here is a monster.

My dog, Hairy!

Karate Kids

Point to the kids who are doing karate moves.
Now point to the kid who is doing something different.

Good Sports

Some kids like to do karate. What kinds of activities
do you enjoy?

Shadow Play

Look at the shadows. Which pet made each shadow?

Little Riddles

What action word that you do on one foot rhymes with **chop**?

What word that you say on Halloween rhymes with **kick**? *(Here's a hint: It's not a treat.)*

What word that tells the time rhymes with **block**?

Terrific Me!

Finish these sentences:

I am as fast as _____.

I am as strong as _____.

I am really good at _____.

Karate Action

Here are some action words from this book:

bow	kick
block	chop
jump	run

Can you find these words in the story?

Ask someone to read the story to you. Each time you hear one of these action words, you can do the action!

Answers

(Karate Kids)

This kid is in a ballet position.

(Good Sports)

Answers will vary.

(Shadow Play)

cat   turtle   bird   rabbit   dog

(Little Riddles)

The rhyming answers are *hop*, *trick*, and *clock*.

(Terrific Me)

Answers will vary.